ELLIPSE

John Van Geem

ISBN: 978-1-952263-02-6

Dedicated to Pyotr Ilyich Tchaikovsky

"Science cannot solve the ultimate mystery of nature. And that is because, in the last analysis, we ourselves are a part of the mystery that we are trying to solve."

-Max Planck

About the Author

John Van Geem is an American Composer, Veteran, and Writer. As an accomplished pianist, John's capacity for music led him to the Chicago College of Performing Arts, where he received his B.M. in Music Composition. With four published albums and hundreds of scores, John's affinity for deep harmonies and unforgettable melodies resonate with audiences all over the world.

Ellipse is John's first novel and acts as the narrative component to the orchestral ballet of the same name. Recorded by the Northwest Florida Symphony Orchestra in 2018, the orchestral score has since been published under "John Van Geem's Ellipse" everywhere digital music is sold.

Lateral to his accomplishments in the Arts, John graduated with an M.A.S. in Space Studies from Embry-Riddle Aeronautical University and is an avid connoisseur of all things aerospace. John currently resides in Washington, D.C., where he continues to compose.

Contents

Page Left Blank Intentionally

Act I

Overture

Moving with a thought, a lone soul resided in the kingdom at the beginning and end of the universe. Its great halls morphed from the ground, while walls of amethyst carried a reflection of the stars.

In the garden of the palace, a vibration began to displace its surroundings. The solitary soul watched on, both witnessing something that never happened, and something that always was.

A violent surge swelled from the landscape outpouring iron and magnesium in a rain of lights. Chromium and aluminum gases followed, adding to the anthology of hypnagogic colors. The surge grew in velocity and strength when the impossible spectra leaped into the sky.

The light became a glimmer, as the faint plasma traversed like a distant star. With a blink, it disappeared. The great halls ceased to grow, and the garden settled in silence...

As the kingdom's sole heir stood waiting; thinking of his father.

The Clouds

The sky transformed as light pierced the horizon, each tree cast in gold from the angle of the sun. Aaron had an affinity for the lesser-known paths and waded through the trees of the forest.

As a teenage boy with a lean build, he would venture out for days without getting tired. His eyes were a frightening shade of blue as if haunted by the ocean. His skin, a result of mid-summer heat, when there was often no reprieve from the sun.

This year's harvest was particularly grueling, requiring extra duties. The farmers relied on him to take the crops to the port, where they were sold to the ship merchants of Eros. If he was lucky, extra profits would ensure him a day off, and yesterday he had come back with coins spare.

The timelessness of the woods healed all of Aaron's burdens. Small droplets of water gathered on the trees, while unnoticeable gossamer caught the light. Wildlife called in every direction, causing Aaron to look up and see a blackbird resting on a branch.

More than any other creature, Aaron was envious of the birds, their ability to fly for miles leaving it all behind, what it would be to see the world from that height, to see the sun breaking over the clouds.

Warm rays broke through the canopy, laying a gentle hand on his back. With an easy sigh, he paused for a moment and refocused directions. A renewed energy led him North, and he embarked towards the rivers that descended from the mountains.

Almost half a day's travel brought him to the sound of the water. He moved through the woods with more energy, when the tree line seceded revealing an immaculate view of the mountains. Edging all the way up towards the river, he stopped to take in the view.

Breathing in deeply, he watched the river pass before him. The water was a conjunction of streams that carried a significant momentum. Unwise to ford against its weight, he knew a safer place a little way up the mountain.

Walking alongside the water, Aaron noticed an unusual gold leaf floating toward him. It swept quickly around rocks, riding the waves of the river. Aaron imagined he was the leaf; swirling left and right, splashing over rapids, and picking up speed, small obstacles became intrepid tribulations, as the water pulled him into an adventure.

The gold leaf drifted further and further away, eventually rounding out of site. Aaron stood in silence for a moment, thinking about where the leaf came from, and where it might be going. Some birds chattered across the water, wondering why he was there.

He regrouped and focused on the crossing a little further upstream. One of his favorite things to do was track smaller streams upriver. He thought finding the water's origin was like walking back through time.

With a little effort, Aaron found what he was looking for and was ready to test his skills. He stuck his hand in to feel the temperature, when his eyes lit up as the water pricked back with an icy jest. He took a moment to plan his route across, and moved towards the water's edge.

On his very first step, a gentle breeze seemed to steal all the warmth from his body. Suppressing a shiver, he continued forward across the shallow rocks. There was a hidden smile on his face and determination in his eyes.

Halfway along the crossing, however, he stopped abruptly. A strange feeling came over him.

Here.

He planted his feet against the current and looked up at the clouds. A delicate balance sang through his body, the weight at his feet, the flowing of the river, and the movement of the clouds. A tranquility rang in the wind... one he had never heard before.

An icy chill bolted up his back, bringing his abstract experience to an abrupt halt. Snapping back to reality, Aaron refocused and continued forward across the river. Avoiding unnecessary falls into the deep water, the ground gradually arose at his feet, and he reached the other side.

He looked up again to see the sun had skipped to an entirely new position. If he headed back now, he would arrive before dusk, but then his grand adventure would be over. Prolonging the inevitable, Aaron decided to go southeast, choosing a circular path back over the way he came. The trail was one he had taken before, and although it wasn't as fun, it was full of interesting flora. His thoughts wandered in and out, as different animals would hear him coming and scurry away. After a while, he recognized a lining of trees that defined the borders between the mountain side and the farms of Tara. The end of the day seemed to harmonize with their glow, and he hardened his emotions to return to responsibilities at the farm.

Aaron arrived Lake Tara, a water basin from the melted ice of the mountains. Taking time to enjoy what would surely be his last moments of serenity, he decided to stay and watch the sunset over the water. Finding a clearing amongst the trees, he relaxed and took a seat in the grass.

As the sun began to dip, an orange and crimson glow filled out over the horizon. Aaron laid back in the grass and took a deep breath. He wished for something else to happen, anything other than his work and responsibilities at the farm. Closing his eyes, Aaron stretched out his legs and his weight faded into the grass. He could see a path unfolding in his mind, slowly taking him back upstream, to the center of the river.

The Rain of Lights

A rumbling caused Aaron to opened his eyes. The sky was dark, and the lake's horizon was indistinguishable from the night. He had fallen asleep. The sweeping bass rolled again, and Aaron slunk with the dread of running home in the rain.

Standing to his feet however, the lack of clouds told a different story, and he was taken aback by the preponderance of stars. It was so clear, constellations reflected off the surface of the water.

Again the reverberations came. Aaron listened carefully, tracking the sound as it increased in strength, and then faded away. Moving with short steps, he felt an unusual sensation at his feet.

Is this an Earthquake?

Something was off, if it was an earthquake, it would be the first one in Tara. Not only that, but the thunder seemed to travel, passing over the land.

It began again, quiet at first, and then with a swell. Aaron struck a defensive posture and the trees began to shake. A strident roar released, and his surroundings illuminated around him. A flash of light followed by a ferocious roar knocked Aaron off his feet. Momentarily blinded, he thrashed in the dirt with his hands over his eyes. The light rattled inside his head, slowly changing to the dark hues of the night. Squinting towards the water, he refocused on the ground, and slowly looked up over the lake.

A fiery light with earsplitting shockwaves blazed a turquoise trail across the sky. Deafening sounds ripped through the air, shaking the branches off the trees. As Aaron gained his footing, barrages of new lights descended all over Tara.

Molten streams of ammolite left disintegrating trails of silver in their wake. Aaron felt small and insignificant compared to the thrashing of the roars. A mayhem of lights bombarded the sky, illuminating the forest with — BOOM — a distinct blast rippled across the lake, and a forceful shockwave slammed into Aaron's body.

The extreme contrast of darkness and light obscured Aaron's orientation. His heart was pounding and he had to find safety, but he couldn't be sure which way to go. He began to run towards the mountains, feeling an irrational sensation of energy and speed with every step.

A pandemonium of birds swooped between the trees, but there was little to shield them as brilliant streaks of fiery gold seared through the sky.

Is this an attack?!

Wildly tripping over obscurities in the dark, Aaron continued to sprint towards the river. He could feel his muscles strain, but his adrenaline pushed him forward.

The end of the valley brought him to a new path. He sprinted with all his might, feeling chaos descend all around him. The more he ran, the more he noticed the rain of lights had a reaction with the air, changing its spectra and colors with vehement roars.

Everything in his body told him to reach the river, and the silhouettes of fading trees meant he was almost there. Sliding to a halt, his surroundings began to illuminate once more. An immense explosion of iron and turquoise splintered the ground, and in a frozen moment, Aaron was blasted off his feet and thrown backwards through the woods.

***

An ear-deafening buzz swarmed in Aaron's head. His right side was all scraped and deep aches hummed all over his body; all Aaron could feel was pain. His clothes had torn where he slid across the rocks; his only appeasement was not being able to see the wounds.

Stillness returned to the mountains, but the calmness was unsettling. Faint embers burned in the distance, as the sound of the babbling river came into focus. Aaron squinted at the water, not sure if he could trust his eyes. The river had split in two, avoiding a mound of new land at its center.

As Aaron stood up, he noticed a strange distortion in the air. It flexed and contracted, shaking his perception of length and scale; almost like distant itself was no longer a constant.

Aaron found himself wading in the water before he even knew what was happening. He was a outside observer while his own body continued through the water. Trudging through the current, the ice-cold water nipped at his skin, but did not induce desire for a retreat.

Aaron slowly took a step on the newly formed mound at the center of the river. A thick haze of dark blue and silver vapor lingered in the air, when a voice, both quiet and smooth, broke from behind the smoke.

"Lasant…" the tone whispered, *"Enta ty."*

A young girl smattered with mud emerged from the departing vapors, her long hair parted to uncompromising deep-cut turquoise eyes. Her pale skin was in sharp contrast to the dripping mud, and there were scrapes where her clothes had torn.

Aaron drew in closer, a sense of empathy washing over him as if her pain was his own.

"Aaron," said the girl.

He froze.

"You're here?" she spoke again.

Aaron was stone silent. He had no idea who the girl was, nor how to respond. He stuttered over his thoughts. Despite being bruised and covered in mud, she was undeniably attractive.

Braking off her gaze, she walked around the mound, continuing to observe the water in the night. Aaron stared are her dumb-stricken and afflicted, when a cold rush of water lapped against his feet. The mound had begun to corrode, and the river charged the mound retaking its position.

"Come on," said Aaron, reaching for the girl to follow.

Taking her hand, they rushed towards the riverside. Aaron's pulse pounded as he pushed through the current. The water stung on his fresh bruises and required much more effort than crossing before.

Looking back, he saw the last of the mound being washed away, and held on tighter to get her across. The depth began to shallow, and Aaron stumbled onshore, with the girl short behind.

"Who are you?" she said.

Aaron looked around, he clearly remembered her saying his name already, but they were alone in the valley. A feeling of unease came over him, followed by a stream of unanswered questions.

Who is this? Does she know me? Did I run into danger... the explosion.

"Did I run towards danger?" said the girl. "What was that explosion?"

Aaron turned suspiciously. He could see a slow realization transform over her face, appearing to understand something he didn't. He suddenly felt in danger, like she knew everything about him.

What's going on here?

"What's going on here?!" the girl exclaimed.

This was too much for Aaron, how was she doing this, she wasn't just copying him, she was reading his thoughts. His adrenaline pumped, and he drew erratic breaths. He just needed some time to think.

"I just need some time to think," she stated.

His panic boiled over, wanting it all to cease, Aaron closed his eyes... *STOP!*

A brief moment of silence succumbed to the gentle babbling of the river. Aaron opened his eyes and saw the girl standing squarely before him.

"My name is *Aura.*

Passacaglia

Aura... there was something about her now; a calming presence. Aaron's heart rate began to slow, and he tapped into the tranquility of the woods.

"Those injuries..." Aaron noticed her back was covered in scrapes. *"We should go. I can make you an ointment for those scrapes and bruises, but we'd have to get back to my farm."*

Aura didn't respond. She stood silently, unfazed by pain, looking disconnectedly out onto the river. Aaron walked to her side, "Come, please. Nothing around here is going to help."

There was no response when Aaron started to say something again, Aura interjected.

"Let's go."

Aaron nodded, and they made their way back into the woods. They traveled mainly in darkness, as the moonlight shown through few breaks in the trees. Fortunately, Aaron knew the path well.

"Are you from Tara?" asked Aaron. "Have we met before?"

He didn't want to pry, but it was going to be a long walk in silence if he didn't.

"I am Tara, yes."

Aaron noticed her far-off tone and surmised she was more frazzled from the explosion than he'd thought.

Their travel was laden with emptiness; Aaron wanted to help Aura, but he was always annoyed when strangers gave empathetic condolences. He did wish he could provide some form of comfort, however. It was then he saw gradients of blue lifting along the horizon.

"It should be close to sunrise now," he said reassuringly. There was no reply.

"You knew…" Aura said. "Did you feel it?"

Aaron was caught off guard. "I was already close by… I saw the lights, but… "

He paused. He wanted to know what she was thinking, but he was too afraid to ask. His immediate assumption was that she was still shaken up from the blast. He didn't blame her; he was feeling the same way.

A memory of being thrown through the air made him shudder.

"We're close now... you can stay the night after we take care of your bruises. There's an open room you can have to yourself."

She didn't say anything.

As they reached a clearing, they spied the sun breaking over the horizon. Aura gazed at the rapidly changing colors and seemed to whisper something.

Aaron's extended state of adrenaline-fueled adventure had taken its toll. His eyes were getting heavy, and each step seemed to take more energy than the last. When they broke through the edge of the woods, Aaron gave an emotional burst; the farm was in sight.

***

It was midday when Aaron woke in a sweat. Lying in bed, he was recalling the bizarre rain of light of his dreams, when sharp pain coursed his side. Timidly, he reached over and felt the bandages wrapped along his side… it was not a dream.

Chasing wild memories, Aaron remembered the shaking ground, running through a rain of lights, an explosion, and… the girl.

Aaron's muscles tensed, realizing she must be in the next room. Aaron swung out of bed and immediately regretted it. The previously dormant pain awoke the wrath, and it seared all the way up his back. Aaron froze until the pain began to subside, acknowledging the repercussions of reality.

Mustering the nerve, he threw some clothes on and hobbled to the door.

What if she wasn't there?

Despite his wounds, his night being a dream would have been much more plausible. He rounded the corner with apprehension, yet there she was, a young girl asleep. Too perfect. He had never seen anyone like her.

He stepped back into the hallway, and tried to clear his mind while he headed towards the kitchen. *All those lights… who had the answers? Only The Teacher would know.*

Aaron recalled stories of the teacher of Eros. Sailors would often drink, and rumor about the man whom had phenomenological knowledge of the stars. If anyone knew what had happened last night…

"Are you thinking about Eros?" a soft voice spoke from the doorway.

"You're up!" Aaron coughed with surprise. A sudden rush of blood bloomed to his face. "Eros," he repeated, trying to buy some time… "Yes."

He cleared a spot for Aura at the table and began to look for some food. "Do you know anybody there?"

"I do, Eros is home to many."

"I was thinking… have you ever heard of someone called The Teacher?"

"The Astronomer of Eros," Aura said with mild surprise.

"Yea," Aaron replied, "I was thinking about him before you came in."

He grabbed a loaf of bread from the pantry and placed it on the cutting board. "Sailors talk about him all the time, I mean, I hear stories… I think he would know what happened last night…"

"Hmm," said Aura

"Do you know him?"

"We will."

The air around them awkwardly came to a halt. Aaron considered this to be a very forward and strange answer.

"Eros," he said, his focus detracted to someplace far away. "…I always wanted to go there."

"What's stopping you?"

"Money."

"I have money." Aura extended her arm to reveal a handful of silver. Aaron stopped cutting and peered, stunned, and still.

"You can come with me," she offered, placing the pieces back in her torn clothing.

"Well, that would be something." his voice held a modest shock. After some deliberation, he let out a sigh.

"I can't just leave here."

"Can't you?"

Another stillness fell over the room, but this time Aaron's thoughts were pulled by the sound of the birds. His imagination erupted, and he could see all of Eros: the fabled market at the port, the infamous cedar ships of Nonabel, and all of the people.

"Eros, huh?" Aaron was still half-dreaming.

Aura took a large bite of her bread, hiding a face that already knew he was coming.

***

Within two days, Aaron began packing for Eros. If he had not convinced Aura to take time to heal, they would already be on their way. Throwing his bag over his shoulder, he took a final look around.

Is this really happening?

Aura's voice came to him. "You look ready to me… trust in me, we'll be a good team. *"*

Aaron let out an overwhelmed burst of disbelief; He was leaving… he was heading to Eros… and he was doing it all with her.

The Seas

Sunlight glittered off the waves, leaving wisps of silver to break over the rocks. A number of boats were anchored to the harbor, rocking slightly as the daily market settled to a close. Aaron recognized a ship that often brought goods back from Eros. It was large, held three masts, and had its name smelt in iron on the stern: *The ELGIA.*

Aaron surveyed the docks, nervously considering the way forward. He spotted a younger man tossing crates onto a pulley system and hoisting them up to the deck. With the other sailors occupied and out of sight, he decided that this was their chance.

"The ELGIA, what a ship… do you have space for two more?" Aaron called.

The sailor released the rope and examined them with doubt. "The ELGIA doesn't take passengers."

Aura stepped from behind Aaron into the young man's view. "We can pay."

"Well… what's with the bruises?"

Aaron flushed with panic; he didn't consider what two young people leaving the village with black and blue marks might look like.

Aura quickly took charge. "This young man is taking me home. My name is Aura, what's yours?"

The man wasn't convinced, and neither was Aaron, but then an unexpected softness came over the sailor's face, and he fell into Aura's deep-cut turquoise eyes.

"Aah... Aura... yeah... follow me. You'll have to get the word of the Captain."

Aaron shot Aura a questionable look as they made their way onboard. It was majestic, boasting a narrower build than other ships from Eros, the vessel could have easily accommodated a crew of forty. The deck was made of thick wood from Nonabel, a village to the North revered for their eminence. Aaron ran his hand over the rails, imagining all the waters it must have seen.

The young sailor stopped in front of a small room, Aaron assumed to be the captain's quarters. There was a silver inscription on the door written in a strange language he had never seen.

"ENTER," blustered a voice from behind the door.

"Captain," the sailor nodded. "Two wayfarers wishing to travel to Eros."

A broad form stepped into the light. He was a disheveled man with gritty and possessive juvenile eyes.

"This is Aura," the sailor said, pushing her forward. "She says they have money."

Aaron stepped in front of Aura protectively but immediately felt foolish. He met the captain's eyes for just a moment before averting to the silver lettering on the door. When the Captain followed his gaze, Aaron felt Aura sneak something into his pocket. He reached in and pulled out eight pieces of silver.

"Hmph." A smile cracked across the Captain's lips as he snatched the silver from Aaron's hands.

"Keep loading, Matis," said the Captain. "We're casting off as soon as you're done." Without acknowledging them any further, the Captain pocketed the silver and stomped towards the deck out of sight.

"Alright," Matis said, looking at Aaron. "Stay outta the way and stay outta trouble." He guided them out of the Captain's quarters and returned to loading the cargo.

Aaron noticed about ten men attending to various tasks around the ship. The majority of them were at least twice the size of Aaron, with rough beards and succinct expressions.

The captain shouted to the crew, who promptly threw off the ropes. Aaron looked up to see large ivory sails unfurled in the wind. With a sudden lurch, the sails stretched tight, and the ELGIA was on its way.

Aaron spied a man half-covered in soot staring transfixed at Aura. He had been untangling nets but paused mid-task. Aura eyed him for a moment when the man suddenly straightened up and gave her a nod. Aaron was impressed, unsure how they would fare on the trip; he saw Aura's talent for amity as a good sign.

The port of Tara shrunk in the distance as they pulled further out to sea. Aaron wondered if he was making the right decision, but he was beyond return now. The shores of Tara were fast departing, and the ship continued towards unaccounted destiny.

Aaron sighed and took a look back at Aura. Somehow, she had made leaving as simple as walking through the door. He would have followed her anywhere.

Thin wisps of clouds did nothing to mask the endless blues of the sea. The ELGIA sailed with considerable speed, cutting through swells and kicking up mist onto the deck. Aaron breathed in the salty air and was amused by the birds still circling from the coast.

Trying to stay out of the way, Aaron anxiously watched as the crew began different tasks around the ship. Some were sorting out goods, while others worked on the buttressing the foresail.

"How are you feeling?" said Aura. She was enjoying herself quite a bit.

"I'm good, just avoiding Jericks over there." He gestured to one of the larger sailors, who, in return, displayed a surly face. "…Are those new clothes?"

Aura was now in a longer dress, one that went all the way down to her ankles. "Yes! The man by the spices…mmm, Ilyich gave it to me."

Realizing he had never offered her a change of clothes, a pang of guilt loomed over Aaron. He thought about what he could have given her and conceded it definitely wouldn't have been a dress.

"It should take six days to get there." Aaron changed the topic. He tried to put on a hardy sailor demeanor, but Aura saw right through it.

"It is usually fourteen days journey for the ELGIA to make a round trip."

"Six days it is then," Aura said smiling.

"We might have to eventually put in some work. I don't imagine the Captain will let us stand around forever."

"Oh, it's no problem," Aura said. "I talked to Matis, so long as we don't drink the Captain's ale, we can have the corner room in the hull next to the spices."

Aaron wasn't used to this sort of luck. In fact, he really wasn't sure what was going on at all. Sailors would frequently catch Aura's eye, stop what they were doing, and proceed to complete the other tasks. It was like she had a strange authority over them, without ever changing her demeanor.

Aaron wondered if she had always effected people this way, and then remembered how dumbstruck and afflicted he was when they first met.

After an hour's work, the Captain resurfaced from the hull. His broad shoulders swung around the deck, casting suspicious looks at his men, as he surveyed their actions. Following a foreboding pause, he set his eyes on Aaron and Aura and began to approach them with intimidating strides.

"Well now," he bellowed in his booming voice. "If I didn't know that these were my men, I could have sworn they were yours." He leaned so close to Aura that she stumbled backward.

"They're doing a better job than I could've gotten them to do... I'll give you that." He wiped some sweat from his forehead and turned to fixed his gaze on Aaron.

Aaron's chest grew tight, and his awkwardness was palpable. "I was wondering... What does the silver lettering say etched on your door?"

The Captain's presence changed from cantankerous to contemplative. He looked at them with nostalgia, while a slight twinkle of perspective changed in his eyes.

In a lighthearted and expedient manner, the Captain said, *"ELGIA lore lasant, enta ty...* it means... *The horizon of your love has no end."*

Aaron's eyes lit up as he looked at the Captain, who smiled wide.

Breaking into a chuckle, the Captain mused, "Hmmmm, yes. I know it's rather girly, isn't it? What can I say... it came with the ship."

The Stars

The ELGIA transited the endless waters, crossing under clouds made of quick wisps of pearl. By the fourth day, untidy strangers became untidy comrades, and Aaron's anxieties faded in the wake of the ship.

For the most part, Aaron and Aura kept to themselves. Every once in a while, Ilyich or Matis would ask Aaron for his assistance, but it was more for Aaron's interest than their own. Men passed the time by playing card games under the deck, while general schedules persisted throughout the day.

Aaron learned how to tie new knots, like the rolling hitch and peripatetic, while Aura was often found in the forecastle peering out to sea.

At twilight, everyone gathered in front of the captain's quarters for the large meal, and at least one barrel of ale. Afterward, it became a habit for Aaron and Aura to survey the horizon and watch the night accede.

"How are my stowaways, the guys aren't messing wi'cha too much, I hope?" The Captain gave Aaron a hearty slap on the back.

Aaron nodded in agreement, satisfied he had not been thrown overboard for sport.

"We appreciate everything, thank you," Aura said, speaking for the both of them. The three of them looked out over the rails and took a moment to take in the stars.

Aaron recognized his chance to ask the Captain some questions; he wanted to know if the rumors were true, or if he should prepare for disappointment. "Captain, have you ever heard of someone they call, The Teacher?"

The deck was quiet, with only the faint chattering of men at the end of their meal.

"See that group of stars over there?" the Captain said, pointing to his upper left.

"Mmm... The Ram?" Aaron replied.

"That's right... the brightest star of that bunch is called *'The First Point of Aries'*... It was The Teacher who first taught me that... he called it celestial navigation."

"He said, when the full cycle saw equal dark and equal light, the sun would align in front of those stars, the planet would be in balance."

"From there, you could map out the whole sky... you have no idea how many times I was able to reorient from that simple piece of information... whatever you want from The Teacher, I'd say he's probably got the answer."

Aaron looked intently at Aura. He wanted to tell the captain about the rain of lights and how they met, but he didn't want to sound crazy. Instead, the three of them stared into the stars, thinking about from whence they came, and from whither they go.

"It's late," the Captain sighed. "The two of you better get some sleep while the waves are still calm."

Aaron nodded but remained in place without movement.

"Goodnight, Captain," Aura said, taking Aaron's arm and kindly guiding him away.

The room next to the spice racks was probably the best spot in the hull. Two cots lined the walls of what used to be a small storage area. Aaron laid in the cot next to Aura, but the possibility of sleeping was thin. He had not slept well since boarding the ship, the closer they got to Eros, the more anxious he became. His longing for answers weighed heavily on his thoughts while he desperately tried to quiet his mind.

ELGIA lore Lesant, enta ty...

Aaron tossed in his sleep, re-adjusting and burying his head. Throwing off his blanket, he looked around to noticed Aura was no longer there. He jostled on some clothes and made his way towards the ladder, ascending to the deck.

As his head reached the surface, a cool breeze rushed across his face. The ship was mostly deserted except for Jericks at the rudder. Aaron walked toward the front of the ship, certain that he would catch Aura at the forecastle.

The sight of the night was magnificent. The cloudless sea exhibited an aggregation of stars, collecting in a silver river across the sky.

"Unbelievable, isn't it?" Aura's smooth voice emerged at his side. He was about to agree when an embarrassing rumble originated from his stomach.

"Guess I should've had more to eat" He rubbed his stomach.

"How about one of these?" a sapphire fruit appeared in her hand.

"Where did you get that?" The situation of her surprising him oddly reminded him of her handful of silver back at the farm. A memory of seeing Aura for the first time exploded in his mind: a think haze of dark blue and silver vapor evaporating to deep-cut turquoise eyes.

The ELGIA dove into a fresh wave and returned Aaron from his daydream.

"You wanted it." Aura replied. "So, take it."

"Yyees…" Aaron agreed with suspicion. He reached out and took the fruit from her hand. It was firm and the same temperature as the ambient air. Aura was clearly hiding something, but he was hungry, so he took a bite nonetheless. It was perfect, probably the best sapphire he'd ever tasted.

"Aura," he began with a mouth full of food, "Where did you get this?"

"I made it," replying as if normal.

"You made it…" Aaron felt he was being pulled into something strange. "How?"

In response to his question, Aura looked towards the sky and raised both her arms into the air. With what seemed like an invisible tug, she rotated her wrist and pulled down with her arms.

An agglomeration of lights lowered from the sky, and gracefully hovered over the deck. It was as though the stars had descended to become a thick layer of luminous motes. Different whites, yellows, and blues drifted about the ship, floating along as if transported by an invisible water.

Amidst the deck of the ELGIA, Aaron was standing in the middle of the stars. Lights brushed past his eyes and swirled into a congregation behind the foremast. Then, with a gentle lift of her palm, the stars returned to their rightful places in the sky, and the ELGIA continued sailing as if nothing had happened.

Aaron wasn't breathing. Although Aura enjoyed the look of shock on his face, she steadily grew concerned and nudged him in the stomach to cue a gasp of air.

"Whaaat!?"

"You wanted me to show you..."

There was an uncomfortable silence as Aaron began to pinch his arms. He might have felt some pain, but he was too deep in shock to notice.

"Maybe Aaa... maybe aaa." Aaron was confident he had lost his mind.

"Would you like some more?" Aura held out the sapphire fruit as if this would resolve the matter. Aaron's eyes grew wide with fear.

"You know, you don't look so good."

Aaron's hands began to tingle.

"Maybe you should get some sleep." Aura placed her hand on his back, in what would have been a comforting manner.

Deliberating on what action would restore his sanity, he agreed some sleep was probably wise.

"Okay."

Aaron descended awkwardly to the lower level with Aura close behind. Rounding the spice racks, he laid down in his cot, careful not to bang his head. His heart was pounding out of his chest, when Aura came in to lay down in her cot beside him.

"Good night, Aura," Aaron said, testing to see if reality still worked the same way he remembered.

"Good night, Aaron," she assured him it did.

The Teacher

Aaron woke to a barrage of footsteps. It was too early for this type of noise, but the clammer continued. Two crew members rushed by his room when Aaron vehemently threw off his blanket and bounded out of bed; the ELGIA had arrived in Eros.

Tripping around in the dark, Aaron quickly grabbed his things and tossed his bag over his shoulder. Climbing the ladder to the surface, Aaron opened the hatch and was temporarily blinded by the light. He stepped onto the deck, shielding his eyes, and slowly squinted into the horizon.

Magnificent vanilla sails waved above the port of Eros, as more than twenty vessels jockeyed for position. Huge ships from Nonabel dwarfed the ELGIA while the Captain could be heard yelling at the crew.

As a large vessel cleared the way, Aaron was consecrated with his first vista of the city. The market alongside the dock exploded with a myriad of banners and flags, each representing a seller of different foods, drinks, and merchandise.

Aaron spotted Aura leaning over the railing and ran over, jumping the center banister and sliding to a halt. It was a picture of pure enchantment.

"You ready?!" Aaron smiled. They both leaned back as another large ship sailed between them and the docks.

Birds flew overhead as the ship glided parallel into position. Aaron's excitement was so perceptible; even the Captain broke into a restrained smile.

The Captain yelled for the anchor to be dropped, and Jericks released the wedge freeing the chains. After four men threw ropes over to the dockhands, the ELGIA was quickly secured.

Aaron and Aura ducked and dove through the crew, racing their way to the ramp. At the boundary of the movable plank, Aaron drew a final glance at Aura and took his first step off the ship.

Eros was a tumult of peripatetic commerce. The market fumed of cardamom and chili, while throngs of patrons jostled in the streets. To prevent becoming separated, Aaron reached for Aura's hand, consequently making navigation through the crowds even more difficult.

To his right, a purple fabric stand was lined with coats and furs from exotic realms. A thin, bearded man stood behind the table, exchanging tenacious looks with a competitor across the aisle.

"Two for one!" yelled another villager the next stall over, selling birds as big as his head. It was nearly impossible for Aaron to walk without bumping into people.

"Euclidian roots! Get your fresh roots!" A voice burst from behind them. Aaron was overwhelmed in the best way. He ogled at everything he saw, tugging on Aura's arm as they pushed through the crowds.

"Pocket Scopes! See the stars in a brand new way!"

Aaron's mind reeled back to the stars floating on the deck of the ELGIA... *Did that really happen...*

"Snargle Pods, five for a dozen!".

Aura spotted an opening and tugged on Aaron. The two weaved their way along the water into the heart of the city. Passing a vegetable stand, alehouse, jewelry booth, medical store, horse stable, and a butcher, Aaron managed to only bump a few shoulders before reaching a break in the crowd.

A new fragrance lofted in the air, Aaron looked around, but couldn't match any of the shops with its origin. Aura caught the scent and pulled Aaron through a small alley. The smell grew stronger, rounding a corner to a mint doorway, with its windows open to the street.

Beckoning them to approach was a floral shop with verdant charm. Arrangements spread across the room gave off the most pleasing aromas, as vivid displays of delicate flowers lined the walls.

"Hello," said an older woman. "Can I interest you in anything?"

Aaron admired a bed of flowers that exhibited bizarre pedals somewhat like lilies.

"Ooo, yes. Those are nice proto cultures... Just two silvers."

Aura stepped forward and handed over the pieces.

Everything moved like a dream with Aura, but it was all too easy... how quickly he abandoned life in Tara to go on an adventure. Everything he wanted was happening, so why couldn't he just enjoy it?

"What brings you to Eros?" The woman asked, looking at Aaron. "Forgive me for noticing, but you seem to be from out of town, yes?"

Aaron pulled himself together. "We're here to find The Teacher... have you heard of him?"

"The Teacher," she echoed, recalling an old friend. "Of course... of course."

"Do you know where we can find him then?"

"Well, no... I mean... he runs an academy now, up North, but it's far from here, definitely not of walking distance."

Aaron considered this and gauged Aura's reaction.

"Thanks for the flower," Aura smiled and began to leave the shop. Stuck in his thoughts, Aaron gave a half-wave and followed Aura out.

"Not around here..." Aaron muttered to himself.

"Well, you know what that means, don't you?" Aura probed.

Aaron stared inquisitively.

"We'll just have to explore!"

Aaron agreed with a smile, but it was only on the surface. As much as he wanted to trust Aura, too many things were out of place… like where she kept getting all that silver.

Eros was much bigger than Aaron had anticipated, and his enthusiasm began to wane. The people were different here, some were overloaded with strange furs, while others almost had no clothes at all. Aaron would ask if they knew the way to the academy, but either no one knew, or no one cared.

The approaching twilight signaled a change in their adventure from leisurely enjoyment, to ominous defeat. Aaron didn't want to admit it, but they were no closer to finding The Teacher than when they first arrived.

"Should we rest?" Aura asked.

"Yea," Aaron replied dejectedly. His legs were sore from walking, and he didn't have the will to be denied by any more strangers. As the merchants closed up their stands, two lamplighters walked the streets, signaling the imminent approach of night.

A young boy stood on the corner, carrying a bag too heavy for his size. When he set it on the ground to rearrange its contents, he pulled out a thick green book with an interesting silver triangle on the cover.

"What's that?" Aaron asked.

"The real thing, that's what. Take a look." The boy proudly held up a textbook reading: COMPLEX HARMONIES AND THEIR DIRECTIONS IN TIME.

"It's from the Academy see. It's a treatise. This one's on music... how it's in the very language that we speak."

Aura leaned in and cast a sideways look to Aaron. "The Teacher wrote that..."

"Where'd you get it?!" Aaron responded so fast the boy's eyes grew wide with fright.

"I didn't steal it! They gave it to me!"

Aaron was confused, but quickly realized he was talking to a troublemaker. "Relax, I didn't say that you stole it. I just wanted to know the directions to the Academy."

"Eeee..." The boy fixed on Aaron, scrutinizing his face for signs of deception. "Okay."

"It's about three hours from here, but you can only get there by horse. Exit north through the city and follow the main route to Tritaselo Pass… that's the only one to the bluffs. Once the pines get thick, you'll see markers for The Academy."

Aaron shot a smile at Aura and handed the book back to the boy. Immediately turning on his heel, the two of them headed back towards the center of the city.

Aaron shouted over his shoulder with brotherly reverence, "Don't steal things!"

They moved quickly across Eros, making way to the stables near the port. Twilight was almost over, leaving only purple and lavender clouds left to fall to the night when they finally stopped in front of the banner that read: *WEST EROS STABLES*.

A rather large man loomed behind the gate, shoveling out hay with a fork. "Be right with you," he called bluntly.

"Getting late, ay… what do you want?"

"We came for a horse," Aaron said.

"Come back tomorrow; it's late." The burly man went back to shoveling hay and ignored them. A few seconds passed when he noticed they weren't giving up.

"Fine. How many?"

"Just one," Aura said, extending another handful of silver. The man quickly changed his attitude and welcomed them in.

"Just a moment, let me see who's ready." A few minutes passed, and he returned around the corner with a stunning Erosian Black Hair.

"This is Peridot... the eyes... she's one of our best, just don't let her eat everything she sees."

Aaron walked around the horse and laid his hand on her side. Her deep breaths raised Aaron's arm as she stomped her front leg against the ground.

Aaron mounted Peridot and extended Aura his hand. In that instant, he saw something deep within Aura's eyes: everything was her; the stable, the horse, his arm, her face... everything was an extension of Aura...

With a bray from Peridot, Aaron was wrenched back to reality. He took a deep breath and hoisted Aura onto the saddle. With a quick kick, they exited the stables and cantered down the road.

Galloping down the streets of Eros, Aura held tight around Aaron's waist. Both of them were eager to reach the Academy, but Aaron noticed fewer and fewer street lanterns providing light.

"We might be too late," Aaron shouted over his shoulder. "It's getting too dark to see."

Aura began to adjust behind him, and with a closed fist, raised her right arm in the air. When she opened her hand, light burst through her caged fingers and illuminated the path in front of them. The bright emission continued to hover above their heads, while Aura returned her arms around Aaron's body.

Aaron didn't even want to look; he continued galloping on, knowing full well Aura had done something impossible. Nevertheless, it was too much to sort out in his head, either he was crazy, or Aura had done something unimaginable, and neither case reconciled with his sensibility.

Instead, Aaron focused on riding, and the hours passed like a dream. Peridot was a joy as they wound their way through the countryside and up the Tritaselo Pass. Once Aaron noticed the pine trees thickening, he abated their travels to a four-beat walk. An unusually thick pine tree stood at the left of a fork in the road. Aaron pulled back on the reins, noticing its trimmed trunk bore some sort of marking at the base. As they moved in closer, Aaron saw a triangle that circled around itself.

"There, that's the sign of the Academy."

He looked up the trail and patted Peridot's side. With a swift kick, they ascended the hill in the direction of the bluffs.

Just as Peridot neared exhaustion, a man-made structure rose along the horizon, its prominence grew in length, spreading wide along the edge of the bluff. Covered with thick vines, the whole building seemed to glow in the night.

Indeed the moons had risen, and waves could be heard crashing against the cliff. Aaron realized he had no idea what to expect, and his nervousness began to rise. Stopping Peridot in front of the entrance, he motioned for Aura to slide off, and they both dismounted securing Peridot's reins.

Contemplating his next decision, Aaron knew there was only one way forward. A few daunting steps towards the entrance exposed its ancient and crumbling facade. Standing one step in front of the door, a familiar silver triangle glimmered in the light. Aura gave Aaron a reassuring look, and he banged three times with the side of his fist. They waited in uneasy silence while waves struck against the bluffs. Aaron went to lift his arm when a latch sprung from behind the thick wooden door. The entrance dislodged from its frame and opened inward towards a candlelit foyer.

A bald-headed man with a neutral face appeared in the opening, wearing a long gray robe that descended to his feet. A peaceful sentry, he stared emptily at them, causing Aaron to swallow his nerves. With the slightest of nods, the bald man motioned for their entrance, and Aaron and Aura stepped in.

Open saucers of oil lit their way around the foyer, as they moved towards the back of the room. The three walked in silence, their footsteps echoing softly against the walls. Descending into a dreadfully dark staircase, Aaron's apprehensions grew vexing.

A circular room revealed itself in elegant gray and white marble. As they walked, the brighter ambiance of flickering oil lamps highlighted staggering pedestals throughout the room. Displayed on each pedestal was a metallic and geometric sculpture, contrasting boldly against the ancient stone and marble in the walls. Aaron reached out to touch one when he heard advancing steps.

"Well, it's not often we receive visitors in the middle of the night." A tall, dark man in grey robes entered the room.

Aaron could see Aura's unique beauty was pulling this man's attention, but the interaction between him and Aura was different. He wasn't being swayed or charmed by her. Instead, he walked about her in a wide circle, scrutinizing her presence. Though Aura remained poised and unwavering, beneath her surface was concern. The man quickly pivoted and snapped his eyes on Aaron.

Aaron could feel the weight of a boulder upon him. His thoughts raced quickly to block and repel the intensity, "Sorry for arriving in the night... we came to find The Teacher... are we in the right place... the Academy?"

The man turned to his helper and gave him instructions with his eyes.

"Follow me."

Aaron was sure this was the man. Following a new passageway, Aaron thought he could still hear the crashing of the waves as they walked parallel to the bluffs. They entered a new room, and Aaron found himself in awe. A library at least three stories tall opened before him with brightly illuminated scrolls on display. Aaron had never seen so many writings in one place.

"I am The Teacher, and this is the Athenæum... what was so important for you to come here in the middle of the night?"

"I wanted..." Aaron's voice trailed off.

The Teacher had seen this look a thousand times. "Yes, my students often get lost in this room as well. If you have the discipline, it can teach you many things. More often than not, however, it remains the vestige of better men."

Aaron took a moment to look at Aura and drew forth determination. "There was... a rain of lights, about a week ago..."

"You're from Tara!" The Teacher interrupted.

"Yes," Aaron recoiled in surprise. He was astonished that The Teacher even knew of the place. "I was in the forest when the rain of lights began. After I had been thrown by a blast, I found Aura in the river."

"You certainly did," The Teacher chuckled. He paused for a moment, then continued to walk around the library. He looked like he had something to say, but wasn't sure how to say it.

"You came because you thought I had the answers about the rain of lights... but now, what you really want answers for... is her."

Aaron was thrown off guard. He did have questions about Aura, and for his sanity he needed some answers. As for what he wanted however, it was for someone else to take the reins.

"I must confess," The Teacher continued, "though I think I know what happened that night... the only one who has answers about Aura...is you."

Aaron looked at Aura, who seemed as confused as he was. "No. You don't understand. Aura can... Aura can do things... she can... make light."

The Teacher looked straight through Aaron, seeing through his every choice.

"Aura is not the one who is making light."

Aaron was getting upset. He had not come here to play word games or philosophize about cause and effect. He wanted answers.

The Teacher recognized Aaron's frustration and stepped in front of him to ensure his message was received. *"Aura is an Einai... she is... energy without form."*

Aaron's muscles began to lock.

"Aura is ... as you call her, a reflection. When an *Einai* comes in contact with a Human, it turns into *Ousia,* that is to say, it becomes the substance form of the human's imagination...you see...Aura is the manifestation of your thoughts."

Aaron's face shifted through various shades of white. He looked at Aura in panic. *She's there... she's not energy... she's normal...well, not normal... but definitely...*

"Aaron... why don't you follow me?" The Teacher gestured towards a den at the corner of the library.

"Just you and I."

Aaron didn't move. It wasn't panic, but shock. He had forgotten how to walk. Taking a step forward, he began to follow the teacher, unable to process whether any of his actions were the right choice. He crossed the library and stepped into the corner den. Right before he entering the room, he looked back to see an uncompromising glimpse of deep-cut turquoise eyes.

The den provided a warmth and comfort that Aaron had not known for a long time. A smokestack with fire merrily cracked in the corner, giving off the smell of charred wood and pine. Instead of chairs, cushions lined the walls, and a round circular table sat above the floor with a decorative lantern hanging above.

Aaron took a seat on a rose-colored cushion, and slowly felt some blood sink back into his face. As The Teacher sat down across from him, he let calmness fill the room until it was settled enough to begin.

"Aaron," The Teacher said.

Aaron's nerves spiked. He had never introduced himself, and now it was clear the teacher knew who he was.

"Let's talk about Aura." The Teacher folded his hands. "Aura is without form. She only is what you want her to be. She is, in a sense, your imagination."

Aaron locked in a calm tone of voice, but was screaming on the inside, "She doesn't... exist?"

"Well... not as a girl." The Teacher looked over to the fire. "If you had not found her, or rather, if she had not found you, then Aura would still be a spirit... some say... the spirit... eternal"

How could this be happening right now?

An angry heat rushed through Aaron's neck and up the side of his face.

The Teacher reached out and touched Aaron's shoulder. "Take a moment, Aaron. Just think about your time with the *Einai*... Aura. Were there times when she reflected your own thoughts, or where she simply produced something you require?"

A flow reversed directions in Aaron's mind, and he was pulled to a new place he would never leave.

It was just as he said...

Paramours

The fire continued cracking in the corner, providing Aaron with minimum comfort as he reckoned with his thoughts. The Teacher gently stood up, made his way to the door, and left Aaron to find his own resolve.

"Aaron!" Aura called from the library.

Aaron did not answer. How could he possibly respond? He could hear Aura's footsteps approaching the door, and took a deep breath as if he were about to dive underwater.

"Let's get out of here," said Aura.

She stood in the doorway, waiting for his response, but Aaron didn't want to look. He didn't want what The Teacher said to be true. Apparently however, the only way forward was headfirst into his fears.

Aaron stood up and looked Aura in the eyes. Her beauty was staggering, but now with great concern, Aaron considered why. Internally wishing he never listened to The Teacher, Aaron swiftly broke contact and advanced to leave the room. He brushed past Aura without a second glance and moved through the library.

Nearly at a sprint, he passed the circular room and ascended the stairs, outpacing the speed of his own shadow. Desperately trying to escape, Aaron sought the grace of the woods, if only to quiet his own affliction.

Aaron burst through the thick wooden doors and slowed only when his lungs drew in the crisp cold air. Walking over to Peridot, the breeze felt good on his face, and he began to untie her from the tree. It wasn't until he mounted when he realized he had no place to go.

"We can go anywhere," said Aura, stepping out of the entrance. "If you let me."

Avoiding eye contact, Aaron trotted over to the entrance and swept Aura onto the horse without saying a word. He gave Peridot a kick, and they galloped down the hill away from the bluff. The ground was barely visible as he raced through the moonlight.

It's too much...

Aaron pulled back on the reins, and they came to a halt. He could feel Aura release her grip around him and dismounted the back of the horse. Aaron sat in silence for a moment and then dismounted in the darkness beside her.

"The Teacher thinks you are an entity… an energy… that you're just a manifestation of my thoughts."

Aura didn't make a sound.

"He thinks that you don't exist, that you're just a spirit, and… and that…" he let out a sigh, "you don't have long hair or turquoise eyes… you only have them because it's what I wish to see."

"You wish to see a girl like me?"

Aaron was not ready for this… *"Are you a girl like you?"*

The two stood in silence, waiting on edge for an answer that would never come. Whatever Aaron was hoping for… it was only him.

"The ELGIA… the stars on the deck… was that real?" Aaron heard the desperation in his own voice.

A sinking feeling began to take hold, as he surveyed Aura in the dark. Even in his anger, her elegance overthrew his capacity for indignation.

I can't… she's not real.

Aaron turned away and stared into the woods. It was almost pitch black when her voice finally came forth with an answer.

"I can show you."

An infallible touch rested on his back, providing reason while soothing his emotions.

"I just want to understand…"

"I'll show you. Imagine something."

Aaron's eyes widened; it was time to sink or swim. "You're going to show me… you mean, you're going to create what I imagine?"

"That is exactly what I'm going to do."

Aaron felt uncomfortable. What he really wanted was for her to say, '*You're crazy*' and '*How could you believe that guy… of course, that's not possible!*'

But she hadn't.

Standing in the dark, Aaron knew there was only one way to find out. He took a step forward and said, "Make us a light."

The ground and flora illuminated all around them. A new silhouette flickered against the trees, and a shadow of Peridot flickered beside it. Aaron slowly rotated to see a fire sparkling merrily between two branches, its flame suspended in the air.

As sure as the fire existed before him, The Teacher had been right. His doubts were vanquished with the darkness. He stepped closer to the fire and felt its warm radiance with his hand. It was as if he had been fighting a current his entire life, and someone showed him the way was downstream.

"You are *Einai*?"

"*Einai* is what some people call me... you call me Aura."

Aaron straightened up. "You said that you would show me."

"Go ahead" encouraging him.

"I imagine a jewelry box... Inside is a stone cut with a thousand facets... the color of this stone is unlike this world, and something no one has ever seen."

Aura's eyes widened as she looked at him with admiration. Reaching out her arm, she rotated her wrist to reveal a small jewelry box.

Aaron didn't even see it happen. It was just there in a blink—a box about the length of her hand.

Aaron reached for it, knowing things would never be the same. He held the box against the light of the fire and examined its design. Placing his thumbs along its wooden seam, he flipped the lid.

An impossibly brilliant gem sparkled with colors that no words could lament. Holding the stone between his thumb and forefinger, the resplendent spectacle of rays danced within the thousand-faceted gem.

"I thought I was asking for something impossible." He admitted, looking at Aura, who stood illuminated amongst the light of the fire.

"Is there something impossible..."

Aaron thought there was going to be an answer, but she just looked at him in silence. If this was his chance to test her... what more could he possibly imagine?

He thought of Tara, the ELGIA, Eros, and the Academy, and that's when what he desired most came to the forefront.

"I want you to create us a home," He said resolutely. "Make it here… strong enough to protect the richest man and large enough for a family. Make it constructed around a fresh spring, where available water is plenty, and a centerfire can provide warmth and cooking."

Aura stood in balance, unmoving and pensive. With a serene expression, she rotated her wrists towards the sky. A cool wind blew across Aaron's face when a familiar rumbling grabbed his attention.

An unusual radiance began to glow around Aura's arms, while the ground shook beneath their feet. In a blink, Aura's body became a source of light and a pulse of energy shot from her palms.

One after another, successive pulses ascended into the air and hovered above the trees. At once, the pulses descended upon the land imagined by him, and Aaron realized there were no limits.

More pulses ascended from Aura's hands in every imaginable color. Streams of light flung past Aaron's head when he realized had seen this before. The flashes of light, the roaring colors…

The rain of lights… it was Aura.

The now incredibly radiant object illuminating the surrounding woods was Aura. The light that streamed from her palms was blinding, and traveled through the air in great waves before descending to the ground.

Aaron noticed the beginnings of physical walls, as magnesium and azure flames soared into the sky. A wild wind kicked up everything not rooted in the ground, and Aaron's heart pounded as a cottage took shape right before his eyes. With a last flash of rhodonite, the night returned to darkness save the lone fire suspended in an atmosphere of dust.

Aaron heard Aura fall to the ground and tried to find her amongst the dust. When the particles had settled, a haze of dark blue and silver evaporated, And Aaron saw Aura lying on the ground.

"Aura, are you alright?"

Just then, A babbling brook trickled its way past Aaron's feet.

Aaron turned to see a two-story cottage composed of petrified wood and amethyst standing before him. A stream flowed through the middle of the cottage and down the front of the trail.

It exceeded what Aaron could have imagined.

"Is that enough?" Aura said softly.

Aaron began to tear. It was overwhelming, crazy, and perfect. He wiped his eyes, trying to hide his face from Aura.

"You might not be human… or even what you appear… but you are more, much more… than my own imagination."

A smile broke across Aura's face, and Aaron felt relief. Aura's smile always made him feel better; it was a whole other miracle of its own.

Aaron stood looking at the cottage, awestruck, and flabbergasted.

"There's one more thing…" Aura looked at him

Aaron was certain there was much more than that.

"I can take you places." Her smile transitioned.

"I know, I followed you all the way to Eros."

Aura shook her head. "Yes, but I can take you places... instantly."

There was a moment of silence.

"Instantly?" Aaron replied. "To where? ...Where would you take me?"

"Anywhere you want... anywhere you can imagine."

Aaron stood in silence, gazing in wonder at the materialized cottage. He wanted to rebuttal and doubt her, but he looked at everything else she accomplished, and could not deny he already believed.

"What if I imagine us to the bottom of the sea? Won't we be in trouble... you know, us humans need to breathe, right?"

"I would never hurt you. That is not what I'm here to do."

Chills ran through Aaron's body. He suddenly realized that she had a reason, a purpose of her own for being here. She had been guiding him to this moment, and to an understanding of who she is.

"You want to go somewhere... don't you?"

"Yes," Aura said, with a galaxy in her eyes. "My home.

Transformation

Aaron's face flickered in the light of the fire. "You're not human!"

"I am a part of all humans," she said with a coyness aimed to sway Aaron to her side.

It was too much for him. He would have followed her anywhere, beyond all that was known... but this was even more.

"Where are we going?"

"There is a kingdom... rested in a nebula, at the beginning and end of the universe. Once you can see it, we can go."

"Once I can see it!?" His disgruntled annoyance rose.

A memory of Aura fast asleep in his farm flooded his mind: a beautiful girl wrapped in blankets he provided. If he had known what she was then... would he have followed?

"Breathe, Aaron."

Aaron's attention turned to the present, and he drew in a deep breath. There was a tingling feeling in his fingers, and he wanted to sit down.

Aaron's grand adventure suddenly felt like a grand trap. He desperately tried to sort out how he had gotten to this point. Was it his idea to seek out the teacher, or was it hers? Aaron thought that Eros was Aura's home... but had she ever said that? He remembered the distrust he felt for Aura in the marketplace, and the pieces fell together.

"Trust me, Aaron."

"I'm not sure how trustworthy you are."

"We work together. You imagine, and I create..."

Aaron looked at the cottage and the babbling stream passing through it.

"You saw it in your mind, didn't you?" Aura spoke softly. "You saw it before it was there."

Aaron reached in his pocket and rolled the thousand-faceted gemstone between his fingers, testing it's physicality.

A gentle breeze blew between the trees. Peridot's front hoof kicked the ground, but then fell back into silence.

"How would we get there?"

"You have to release your imagination."

"My imagination?"

"Yes, to untether yourself from the now."

Aaron took a few steps back.

"...You're holding on to this place with your mind, but you don't have to be here."

Aaron nervously laughed. "You know, that might be a bit difficult for a non-eternal being."

A light sparked in Aura's eyes.

"You imagine what to eat before you eat it, you imagine what clothes to wear before you wear them, and you imagine where to go... before you *get* there."

"How can I imagine a place I have never seen?" he exclaimed. "It's one thing to travel someplace new, but it's entirely different to imagine a place at the beginning and end of the universe."

Aaron rubbed his temples. Why was his world being constantly turned upside-down? Where was the sanity?

"Come sit with me," a new tranquility arose in Aura's voice.

Aaron continued to rub his face. This was absurd, if The Teacher was right, and Aura was a product of his imagination, then why would he be fighting about what was possible?

Aura waved her hand, and a ripple of pacification passed through the woods. Aaron became a disembodied observer, watching his legs walk, stop in front of her, and sit on the ground. This had happened to Aaron once before, when he found himself wading in the middle of an ice cold river.

"Close your eyes, Aaron." Aura's words echoed in his mind.

Aaron closed his eyes and sat alone in the dark. His breaths felt heavy, and his attention turned towards the beating of his heart. *What am I doing? Is she going to tell me where we're going? ...Where are we going? We're going to a Kingdom... The Kingdom at the beginning and end... it's a palace, sitting on a nebula, amidst a trillion stars...*

He saw it.

He wanted to speak, but there was no need. A connection existed between him and Aura that transcended words. A fluid conversation of emotions flowed between them like a river, channeling all his anxieties, anger, and longing at the same time.

I Will Always

An immense wave reversed the stream, and Aaron felt the pacification of Aura.

At this moment, Aaron understood the exactitude of his purpose. He knew who he was, and who they would become together; they were a team and would travel the universe side by side.

Aaron disconnected from Aura and opened his eyes. For a timeless second, they both sat staring at each other without saying a word.

A few breaths later, he stood up, walked to Peridot, and untied her from the tree. Rubbing his hand across her side, he took one last look around.

"Well... I suppose I should untether then."

He removed his hand from Peridot's side and walked towards Aura as she rose from the ground. Once again standing face to face, Aura stepped into him and leaned against his chest. Aaron slowly wrapped his arms around

Aura, and focused on her, as though he were witnessing a miracle. Aaron could feel a warm glow emanating from his chest, the same glow he observed from Aura. A distortion reverberated isotropically through the air around them, expanding and contracting, changing the distance between all things.

Let me…

An invisible force pushed them from all sides, accelerating them in a direction Aaron had never felt before. The dynamo sparked flashes of light that whipped around them, diving in and out of sight.

Aaron tucked his head into Aura's embrace, resting the side of his cheek against her hair. He could feel terra firma slip from under his feet like sand through a sieve. The wind roared in the shape of a sphere, and a deep tremble shook the atmosphere around them.

The wind kicked up dust that turned to sparks of light as Iron and Magnesium plasma illuminated the air. The more Aaron untethered, the more visceral the lights became. Aura dug her head into Aaron's chest even tighter, and a new wave of chaos erupted in plasma.

The intensity was becoming too much to bear. Ammolite and silver swirls turned into turquoise flares, as his existence disorientated. His desperate embrace with Aura was the only constant of time.

Reaching an apex of velocity, the deafening roars began to recede. Silver and azure plasma decayed into gold, and the lights slowly transformed back into wind. When the ground returned to his feet, Aaron looked to see a dry and cracked regolith. The dust settled, and Aaron let go of his embrace.

Endless lights shone through what looked like a million holes in pink silk. Aaron could feel the warmth of the stars on his skin. It was neither day nor night, but an aduro twilight of stars. When Aaron turned back to Aura, he saw what they came for; Along the regolith fading into the horizon, was a palace amidst a trillion stars.

Its walls of purple amethyst reflected the light of the nebula, giving the impression that it was made of the heavens.

"Well," said Aura.

Aaron remained firmly planted, his locked gaze over the horizon had transfixed him. Indeed, they had arrived at

Aura's home. Gathering the strength to look away from the palace, he placed his eyes back on Aura and reached for her hand.

Aaron felt like he was walking through the cosmos. The audacity of lights was so spectacular he could barely focus. With each step, the palace's imposing structure grew more profound, and a magnificent entrance drew into view.

Admiring the great amethyst gates, Aaron had the striking feeling of someone watching him. His eyes quickly scanned the grand entrance, as a deep chill struck.

At the entrance stood an epic figure presiding over the palace gates, awaiting their arrival.

The Father of Time

Aaron squeezed Aura's hand and heard her expel a breath of laughter. There was nothing to fear, and she proved it by leading him forwards towards the palace steps.

At the top of the entrance was a brooding man draped in an ivory cloak. He had long white hair and a beard that extended to his sternum. Leaning against a staff as tall as his body, the man's thunderous gaze seemed to dilute time itself.

Aaron was nervous, but Aura showed no fear. He had the strange sensation of falling upwards towards the figure, as they ascended the palace stairs. Continuing to ascend, Aura pulled back on Aaron's arm, only ten steps in front of the figure. The man's eyes were a shade of ice blue so brilliant they could have tempered the stars.

"Hello, Aaron, Aura…" An authority quaked over the nebula. *"I am the Dissemination of Eternity… otherwise known as The Father of Time."*

Lowering his hood, the man revealed a pleasant and grandfatherly face. He seemed to appreciate Aaron's blank expression, as his lips pulled tight to stiffen in a smile.

"Welcome to the Kingdom at the Beginning and End of the Universe."

The doors at the top of the stairs opened, unveiling large symmetrical columns in a grand hall. Aaron and Aura walked alongside Eternity as they ascended the steps into the palace.

Crystal columns morphed with slow viscosity into the ceiling, while their amethyst insides sparkled with past stars, like water traveling up the root of a plant.

"I've been looking forward to this moment for a long time," Eternity said as they passed through the hall.

The hall alone was bigger than any structure Aaron had ever seen. A hundred ships could have easily fit between its columns.

"Let me be your guide, Aaron. There is something I would like to show you."

They entered a large elliptical chamber with eleven passageways leading to adjacent corridors. A large opening, half the size of the room, existed in both the ceiling and the floor. Suspended and centered through the openings was a long black cable, with an origin obscured from view.

Aaron walked along the ledge to see what lay below. Four more identical rooms existed, from which the cable descended all the way to the bottom. At the bottom of the cable was a silver mass, swinging gently.

"*Careful now...*" said Eternity.

A pendulum carved wakes in a pool of liquid metal. The wakes did not resolve in a partial differential equation, but remained sustained in static space, until the length of the cable was equal to the distance carved. This resulted in a harmonograph that faded proportionally to time.

He continued, "*the balance of that pendulum is very particular.*"

Eternity moved surprisingly fast. He whisked them into the next room, where the shadow of a tesseract rotated angrily against the walls. Its figure was becoming more perturbed the further they traveled into the room. Eternity again paid no attention, and briskly continued on.

"*Forgive me,*" *he said.* "*There are one hundred and thirty-seven rooms in this palace, but only one I've been waiting for you to see.*"

Eternity led them to a spiral staircase where they descended to the ground floor. Every twelve steps, another intriguing room would branch out, slightly morphing and cascading as distant stars seemed to course like liquid within its walls.

"I have to admit," said Eternity, *"I wasn't sure how I was going to feel about your arrival... I imagine that you have some questions?"*

Aaron looked at Aura, smiling and giving him a look that said: *why not?*

"'The beginning and end'... what does that mean?"

"Mmm, yes, that's a good place to start. Your fellow humans have developed some knowledge of the stars... but they can't understand that as the universe expands, it moves towards its own beginning."

"This Nebula is the focal point of that beginning, and thus stands at the balance of the beginning and end."

They reached the bottom floor and stepped into an atrium that had an open face to the nebula outside.

"This is it, Aaron, the Garden of Time."

Aaron stepped into the garden and understood where the thousand-faceted stone had gotten all its colors. There were even colors he could feel, rather than see with his eyes. A harmony was present, one that could have been easily missed.

"This garden provides the scaffolding of all beings."

The three of them spread out through different paths, enchanted by the garden's virtue and perfection.

"Aaron, I think you deserve some answers, though I'm sure The Teacher did his best."

Aaron looked over at Aura.

"Aura was born of this garden, for no other reason than being a balance of this universe. She is not a person, as you now understand, but the spirit. She is the will behind that which walks amongst the stars."

"Einai?" Aaron's voice cracked.

"Yes, some use that word... though I will say, The Teacher's iterations get a little lost over time."

"So you knew him... You know him?"

"Yes, he has done a lot to secure your future, and the things you will become."

"So, he did know me?" Aaron pondered. "… he knew before I ever even arrived…"

"Yes… Time does not flow as uniform as you see in the river. Once you left your planet, you stepped into an axiom of rivers, all of which branch from this location."

Aaron brushed his hand over a large leaf that morphed in the shade as it bent back into shape.

"For example, if we wanted, we could observe you boarding the ELGIA for the first time… we could also see your future and the things you have yet to accomplish. A discerning mind could even follow along, as one's actions rippled through the universe."

Aaron didn't know if he was impressed or scared. "You're not human, are you… are you like Aura?

Surely he hasn't lived forever…

"Quite right," said Eternity, amused. *"Well, I don't have an age, per se, but I haven't existed forever. I am a little*

different because of my lineage… you see… the Spirit of All Things… Aura… is my Mother."

Ellipse

Aaron wasn't surprised and realized it actually made a sense, or perhaps he was getting used to being upside-down, and another change felt right on cue.

The three continued to walk through the garden. An extraordinary arrangement of colors reverberated around every corner. Aaron saw colors he had never seen, and some colors he had once, in a thousand-faceted stone.

"Spend some time here, Aaron, and when you're ready… I will show you your future." Eternity held a glance of admiration and turned to depart the garden.

Aaron bent over to smell an exotic-looking flower. He felt at ease, a quality he attributed to a place at the beginning and end of the universe. As he inhaled, a tingling sensation ran to the top of his head.

Although he was enthralled by the scale of it all, there was one thought that Aaron couldn't avoid… *What am I doing here?*

A clear view of Aura rose over a multi-spectral hedge. A dew-like vapor ascended in the air around her as she walked amongst the flowers. Aaron watched for a moment, mesmerized by the grace of the garden.

"So, this is your home?" He walked up beside her.

"Yes, do you like it?"

"It's beautiful... but you don't need me to tell you what I think... do you?"

Aura smiled, "It's not what you think, it's your emotions... how you feel."

"Well... I'm grateful to be able to see your home," Aaron replied, smiling.

They continued to walk together, feeling the warmth of the trillion stars as they glided through the gradient flora. It was easy to be around Aura now, and Aaron carried on with her like an old friend.

"I must confess," Aaron continued, "I saw a glimpse of this place when I lifted you up on Peridot at the stables... I mean... It wasn't the garden... but a connection to it all... a connection of light through time."

Aura held up a flower petal that lifted off from her fingers. It fluttered around their heads for a moment and rose to the top of the palace's walls. "Was that me or you? I don't remember," Aura said playfully.

It was all so clear and confusing at the same time. Everywhere Aaron looked, he saw something he had never seen before, yet it felt rooted in everything that always was.

"After The Teacher told me... you know, about how you took the form of my imagination... I was worried that you weren't real... but you're not just my imagination... are you?"

"No," said Aura, "I am my own ousia. I know you were worried... but it was better for you to find out on your own."

Aaron held a look of doubt in his eyes and paused to think. "Couldn't you have just brought me here, to begin with?"

"You think so?!" She laughed. "And what would you have thought of the Kingdom at the Beginning and End of the Universe then?"

"Hmmmm, I guess I see your point."

Aaron thought about the farm back in Tara, and his hikes along the mountainside. He imagined what his former self would have thought about the Garden of Time. He looked back at Aura, who embodied the harmony of her surroundings.

"You know, for a moment I thought I was going to spend the rest of my life with you... That would have been nice... I mean, it's unfortunate that all the work you did will go to waste."

Aura smiled. "We're not trapped here; we can still live there together."

"What? Well then, what does Eternity want with us?"

A few droplets of water hovered over Aura's shoulder and landed on a tree bearing semi-transparent fruit.

"He's waiting to tell you, isn't he?"

Aaron glanced at the Atrium and felt a surge of nervousness. When he looked back at Aura, she was already out of sight, and he was left by himself.

Why am I here?

He began to walk towards the atrium, and his foot scraped across something metallic and smooth. Looking down, he saw some type of engraved plaque covered in topaz colored ivy.

Uncovering it with his hand, he wiped away the leaves and recognized a phrase he had once seen on the Captain's door: '*ELGIA LORE LASANT, ENTA TY.*'

What was it doing here?

Aura came into view as he knelt above the plaque. "Eternity's not going to wait forever."

"You sure about that?" Aaron smiled and rose. Heeding Aura's cue, he gazed one last time amongst the garden.

When Aaron approached the atrium, Eternity was leaning against his staff, watching the amethyst slowly crystallize out of the ground.

"My apologies, Aaron." He stood up straight. *"I shouldn't have enticed you to leave the garden. You could have spent more time there."*

"It's something else… I was wondering though, why do you care who I am?"

"Oooo, Everyone cares who YOU are," Eternity's ice blue eyes caught the stars. *"Come. Follow me."*

They wound their way back through the Atrium and ascended the spiral staircase. When they reached the third floor, Eternity waved his hands and a light without origin illuminated the length of the hall.

"Aaron, what I am about to show you is very old. I brought it here when I was much younger, and I'm glad that I did when I had the chance."

Entering a new room, Aaron was confronted by a towering archway made of Pezzotaite. It was at least four times his height and presented a righteous proportionality.

"This is the Portara," said Eternity.

Aaron nervously swallowed. Eternity walked around the room, followed closely by Aaron. Light refracted off the Pezzotaite, sending particles shimmering in every direction. Both organic and composed, the geometric crystals grew out from the base, and extended the whole length of its sides.

"This archway will take you back to your world."

The Portara didn't seem to lead anywhere however, it being centered in the middle of the amethyst walls. Aaron was about to question Eternity, but thought better of it.

"Aaron, Aura brought you here because it's your responsibility to shape the future. I understand that you think everything is in a reasonable order, but you must consider this: the grand design is designed by no one but yourself."

Aaron didn't really understand what Eternity was telling him.

"Why do I need the gate? Can't I just go back with Aura the same way I came?"

A look of concern fell over Eternity's face. *"I'm afraid that your future is not your past... The Portara is going to take you somewhere you can start over."*

Aaron was getting frustrated, Eternity was clearly leaving out answers, and the enchantment of the palace was fading away as Aaron filled in those missing answers with his own ominous thoughts.

Eternity leaned against his staff as though he bore a great weight, one he had been carrying for a long time. *"It's not just me that you're helping; others will follow in the path you lay."*

Aaron could feel a deep undertone of sadness come from Eternity's voice. He wanted to ask but realized he might not want to know.

"You must learn to place your trust in Aura. She is paramount to your success. There are forces that would wish to undo my work… but if you trust Aura, you will always find yourself at the doorstep of the Kingdom at the Beginning and End."

At this moment, Aaron realized there was danger in his future, and the possibility of never returning. Aaron didn't like what he was being thrown into, but there was little room for choice.

"What are you asking from me?!" Aaron demanded directly.

Eternity looked at him with aged admiration. *"For you to be exactly who you are."*

Aura walked into the room and broke his chain of thought. A comforting smile emanated from her eyes. Aaron thought that as long as he was with her, things would be okay.

"Will I ever see you again?" Aaron asked Eternity, noting something familiar in his face.

"Ooo, I wouldn't ruin the surprise," Eternity chuckled like an old man.

A great sadness weighed on Aaron's chest. He was about to lose something; he could feel it. Was it because he was leaving now, or was it something else? He wanted to stay. Even though his world had turned upside-down, he felt a powerful connection to the palace.

"Aura will accompany you on your adventure, wherever you go."

Aaron didn't know what his future held, but he had the feeling it had already happened. He didn't know why he was feeling so emotional, he had barely been at the palace for a night. What was there for him to be so distraught about?

"Are you ready?"

Aaron was never going to be ready, but he was going to do everything he could. Without any evidence the Portara led anywhere other than the other side of the room, Aaron stepped up to the stone. A quiet and depressing thought touched his heart.

"Will I die?" Aaron asked.

"O, Dad," said Eternity, *"The Horizon of Your Love Has No End."*

And with a brief moment between father and son... Aaron walked through the gate.

JOHN VAN GEEM

Made in the USA
Monee, IL
25 March 2020